Read on if you dare!

Everybody loves a scary story. Now you can enjoy tales that come with a good dose of fright, lots of suspense and a bit of humour too! Phobia books are about all your favourite spooky subjects such as monster aliens, haunted houses, scary dolls and magical powers that go haywire.

COULROPHOBIA

THE FEAR OF CLOWNS

EVERYONE IS AFRAID OF SOMETHING.

You might be afraid of quite a number of things. But a PHOBIA is a very special fear. It is deep and strong and long-lasting. It is hard to explain why people have phobias — sometimes they seem to come out of nowhere.

In this story, Josh has a phobia about clowns. Clowns, with their weird make-up and those wide, toothy grins, are definitely creepy. Unfortunately for Josh, he and his friends end up in a place where clowns are always found. And it's bad enough when Josh finds one . . . but it's even worse when one of the clowns finds him.

1

It started as soon as I sat down at my desk and pulled out my science textbook.

"Put your books away," our teacher, Ms Bentley, said as the bell rang. She wore a huge smile on her face. "We won't be needing any books today. I have a surprise for you."

My heart thumped. There are two things you need to know about me. First, I hate surprises.

Ms Bentley beamed at us. "Every single one of you got a B or higher on the recent maths test," she said. "As a reward, we are going on a field trip."

The whole classroom erupted into excited chatter. Everyone was happy but me.

"Where are we going?" my friend Theo asked.

"I can't tell you. It's a surprise!" Ms Bentley answered. "You'll find out when we get there."

I put my hand up in the air. "But . . . don't we need permission slips from our parents?"

"Great question, Josh!" she said. She waved a packet of envelopes in her hand. "I have all the slips right here."

"What about *our* permission?" I continued. "Don't you need permission from us too? What if we don't want to go?"

All the kids stopped talking at once and turned to glare at me. "Shut it, Kapoor," hissed Trevor, the class bully.

"Trevor McBain, that's not how we talk to people," said Ms Bentley with a frown on her face. "Line up, everyone!"

I shut my mouth and reluctantly got in the line.

We filed out of our classroom to the bus that was taking us to our unknown destination.

Kids were laughing and speculating about where we were going as we climbed onto the bus. I took a seat at the back behind my friends Sienna and Theo. As the bus pulled away from the school, my stomach twisted. I didn't like not knowing where we were going.

Sienna leaned over the back of her seat. Her cheeks were pink and flushed. "Did you hear the news?" she asked.

I shook my head. "What news?"

She stuck her tablet in my face. "Read this!" she said.

A news story was pulled up on the screen, with school pictures of three different children. I frowned.

"What is it?" Theo asked.

I read the story aloud. "The search is still on for three missing children, Zac Perry, aged twelve,

Felicia Johnson, aged nine and Bethany Quam, aged five. The children went missing late last week. Zac was last spotted at the Ritchfield school playground, Felicia was last seen on the swings at Riverside Park and Bethany went missing from her front garden. The children disappeared without a trace, except for one key clue. In each location, police found a deflated balloon."

I gulped. "That's terrible," I muttered.

"Whoa . . ." Theo said.

"Keep reading!" Sienna hissed.

I read on.

"Detectives believe someone dressed as a clown lured the children away with balloons, toys, sweets or other food or treats. Police also believe the suspect had a helper, perhaps another child."

Remember I said there are two things you need to know about me? Here's the second thing – I'm terrified of clowns.

I swallowed and kept reading.

"A person of interest was taken in for questioning late Wednesday night. The suspect remains in police custody."

"Creepy, huh?" Sienna said, reaching for her tablet. The tablet nearly slipped from my sweaty fingers as I handed it back to her.

"It's like something from a horror film!" Theo popped his head over the seat, grinning. He looked almost excited. "Can you believe something like that would happen around here?"

"It's not really around here," Sienna corrected. "Ritchfield is almost a hundred miles away."

"Someone should tell Ms Bentley!" I said. "We really shouldn't be going on a field trip when kids are getting nabbed by some weirdo."

Sienna stared at me, her lips pressed together, and Theo gave me an outright frown. "Didn't you read that article?" he said. "The guy's behind bars."

"Nothing to worry about, Josh," Sienna said. "Relax."

My friends were always telling me to relax. Of the three of us, I was the cautious one, always overthinking everything. Maybe I *should* just relax, I told myself.

I slumped down in my seat and stared out of the window at the bright sunshine. Even though the clown was locked up, the story made me shiver. When I closed my eyes, I imagined what those kids must have seen. A clown, hiding behind face paint and balloons, waiting to strike. *At least it wasn't me,* I told myself.

2

The bus rumbled to a stop at a red light. I glanced out of the window, and what I saw stopped me cold. My heart launched like a rocket into my throat.

A clown stood on the corner, holding a sign reading *Circus Pizza*. He wore an ugly grey-striped suit. Orange hair spiralled from his head, and a red grin was painted across his chalk-white face. His wig bounced as he jumped maniacally, waving at cars as they passed. I stared at his white gloves, my throat tightening. He was like the clown from my

nightmares. I wanted to duck down in my seat, but I couldn't look away.

Then he saw me. Our eyes met. He stopped still and dropped the sign. He stared at the bus. Then he lifted his arm. A white-gloved finger pointed straight at me. "I'll get you," he mouthed.

I collapsed against the back of my seat.

The light turned green. As the bus lurched forward, I lifted my head and peered over the seat out of the back window to see if he was still watching me.

He was still there, staring at the bus. Then he threw his head back and laughed.

I pounded the back of Sienna and Theo's seat. "Hey! Did you see that?" I shouted.

"Yeah," Sienna called back. "That's the new pizza place."

"I've heard it's good," Theo added.

"I mean, did you see the clown?" I said.

"The restaurant has a circus theme," said Sienna. "Seriously, Josh. Just because there was one creepy kidnapper clown, you can't be afraid of *all* clowns."

I sighed. My friends knew I didn't like clowns, but they didn't know how absolutely terrified I was. They didn't know about the nightmare I kept having over and over – a clown leaning over my bed, his white-gloved hands reaching towards my throat. But deep down I knew Sienna was right. I shouldn't be scared of the clown outside the pizza place. He was far behind us now, anyway.

I closed my eyes and tried to get excited about the field trip. Wherever we were going, at least it would be far away from that clown.

When the bus slowed, I finally opened my eyes and saw a Ferris wheel rising into the sky. A lighted sign reading *Welcome to Auguste's*

Amusement Park! blinked on and off. I groaned. Worst nightmare confirmed. Amusement parks are where clowns hang out. It's their habitat. There was no way I was going to make it out alive.

When I didn't budge from my seat, Theo urged, "Come on, Josh. Let's go!" The bus would be leaving soon. I didn't have much of a choice. I stood up and reluctantly shuffled to the front of the bus. The scent of popcorn wafted through the air. It smelled good, but I still didn't want to be here.

Ms Bentley gathered us together outside the park as she passed out admission tickets and passes for all the rides and games. When she approached me, I took a deep breath. I knew my classmates would be angry about what I was going to say.

"Ms Bentley, did you hear about the missing children?" I asked.

She blinked. "I'm glad you brought that up,

Josh," she said. "We didn't want to cancel the trip, but . . ." She raised her voice. "Listen up, class! The amusement park is safe, but we still want you to be very careful! Use the buddy system. Stay together at all times. Don't go anywhere with anyone you don't know. And DO NOT leave the park! Meet back here at 1.45 – sharp!"

Theo and Sienna flanked me as we walked through the park entrance. "I can't wait!" Sienna said, clasping her hands together. "Ferris wheel, popcorn, candyfloss, bumper cars, throwing games–"

"And don't forget the fun house!" Theo interrupted.

Sienna tilted her head towards me and placed a finger on her lips. "There might be *clowns* in there." She giggled.

"Don't make fun of me," I grumbled. "I'm not scared of . . ." I trailed off. Even thinking the word "clown" brought the frizzy-haired monster of my nightmares to mind. I shivered.

"There are plenty of other options," Sienna chattered on.

"Don't worry about it," I said. "I'll do whatever you guys want to do."

I wondered if I would regret those words.

3

Sienna popped a kernel of popcorn into her mouth. "What next?" she said. We'd already gone on every ride: the Ferris wheel, the Tilt-a-Whirl, the Mixer, the miniature roller coaster (which Theo called "boring"), the bumper cars and the carousel. We were out of ride options, and I was starting to feel a little dizzy.

"Let's try some games," I said. I was being brave. I knew that clowns might be lurking in Game Alley, twisting balloons into shapes for little kids or calling for people to try some games. But what could happen in bright sunlight, with my two friends with me? Besides, I'd left the creepiest clown behind, back at that pizza place.

By mid-morning, I was starting to forget all about clowns. I won the ring toss twice and gave my prizes (a teddy bear and a Frisbee) to Theo and Sienna.

"Hey, look," Theo said, pointing. "A dunk tank! Let's give it a try."

I turned in the direction Theo was pointing.

A clown was sitting on the chair that hovered over the dunk tank. *One Ticket to Dunk Bozo!* read the sign above him.

I didn't want to take one step closer to the clown, but I also didn't want my friends to know I was afraid. I took off towards the dunk tank. "I'll get you," I muttered.

Sienna and Theo hurried to keep up. "This is your chance, Josh! Pretend he's the kidnapper," Sienna said.

"Get him good," Theo added.

I handed tickets to the attendant. He gave me three beanbags and explained the rules. I stared at him as he spoke, trying to avoid looking at the clown. "You have three tries," the attendant said. "Aim for that circle. If you hit it, the chair drops, and Bozo plunges into the water."

I nodded and moved in front of the dunk tank. A crowd was gathering to watch.

"Give me all you've got, kid!" jeered Bozo. "Na-na na-na-na!"

I swallowed and looked up, ready to take a good look at the clown, and a good aim too. What I saw stopped my heart.

It was the clown from the pizza place. The same grey striped suit. The same curly hair. The same evil stare. "You!" he snarled.

I threw with all my might.

DING DING DING DING DING!

I hit the target on the first try. The seat collapsed, and the clown splashed into the water.

I felt an amazing sense of relief.

The crowd cheered and laughed. A few kids patted me on the back. After a few minutes, people started moving away, on to other attractions, but I remained rooted to the spot.

The clown still hadn't emerged from the water.

I began to worry. He must have hit his head. He could be drowning! I ran to the other side of the dunk tank to get the attendant. But he wasn't there anymore. I scanned the crowd but didn't see him.

When I turned back to the dunk tank, Sienna and Theo were leaning over it, peering into the water.

Sienna straightened. "Nothing," she whispered. "Just an empty tank."

I moved slowly towards the dunk tank. I didn't want to look, but I had to.

I peeked over the edge. Sienna was right. The clown was gone.

4

"It's gotta be a trick," said Sienna.

"Yeah," said Theo, his mouth full of hotdog, "like a trap door or something." He held out his half-eaten hotdog. "Want some?"

We were sitting at a picnic table several stalls away from the dunk tank. I shook my head at Theo. My stomach hadn't stopped twisting and turning since the tank. I put both elbows on the table and rubbed my head.

"It's a trick, Josh," Sienna repeated.

"Even if it is," I said, "how do you explain the

fact that Bozo is the *exact same clown* from Circus Pizza?"

Sienna and Theo exchanged glances. I knew that look. They thought I was out of my mind. Sure enough, Theo let out a huge sigh. "Because they're not the same," he said.

"Bozo's hair was definitely different. More red than orange," Sienna said.

"I think he's following me," I said quietly.

"Don't be silly," Sienna told me. "It's just your imagination running wild."

I wasn't so sure. Bozo definitely looked like the clown from the pizza place.

"Come on," Sienna said, standing up and chucking her rubbish into a bin. "Let's forget about it and do something fun."

"What about the House of Horrors?" Theo said, pointing ahead. At the very end of the paved street was what looked like an old, abandoned mansion, with uneven turrets and spooky, cracked windows.

A sign outside read *Prepare for a Scare! Enter the House of Horrors If You Dare!*

"Let's go!" I said. This would be a good distraction. I'd been to a lot of haunted houses, so I knew what to expect – ghosts that leap out at you in the dark and wicked laughter coming from all directions.

We got in the queue for tickets. At the entrance, Sienna paused and looked at the attendant, who was dressed like Dracula, fangs and all.

"Are there any clowns in here?" Sienna asked. I dug my elbow into her ribs, but she ignored me.

"None," said Dracula, eyeing her. "None at all."

"Thanks a lot," I muttered to Sienna as we stepped inside.

Sienna shrugged. "Just making sure."

The House of Horrors was like I expected. Glowing ghosts popped out of dark corners. A pile of bones assembled itself into a full, standing skeleton and screamed at us. A coffin opened and revealed a mummy inside. Sienna clutched my arm as we walked past.

"Scared?" I said.

"No," she lied. "I just tripped."

"Yeah, right," cackled a familiar voice behind us.

"Hey, McBain," I said, turning around.

Trevor sneered at me, his teeth glowing in the flickering sconces that lined the walls of the corridor.

"I'll give you something to really be scared about," he said. "I just heard some breaking news. That kidnapper clown escaped from prison, leaving nothing behind except . . ." Trevor moved closer and lowered his voice. ". . . a deflated balloon!"

A chill snaked up my spine.

"You're making that up," Theo accused.

"Totally," Sienna agreed, turning her back on Trevor. "Let's keep moving."

She let go of my arm as we moved into the next room. The room was pitch black. I couldn't see anything. I stood, waiting patiently for something haunted house-like to happen. I thought maybe a glowing phantom would emerge from behind a dark curtain, or a creepy voice would echo from above. But nothing happened. I got the feeling we'd made a wrong turn.

I put my arms out to feel for my friends. "Hey, guys," I said.

No answer.

"Sienna? Theo? Where'd you guys go?" I called.

Not a sound.

I took a couple of steps forward, feeling around in the dark for the wall or a door. All I felt was empty air. I stepped forward again, arms outstretched. Suddenly, my hands touched something warm and soft.

"Looking for me?" a voice hissed.

A torch snapped on, lighting the clown's face from below. He stood so close I felt his breath on my face. For a full second, I stood frozen in place.

He grinned at me with glowing eyes. Then he laughed, revealing a set of sharp teeth dripping with blood. "You found me!" he cackled.

I screamed, and the torch snapped off. Darkness enveloped the room. I stumbled backwards and grasped at the air, trying to feel my way out.

My fingers brushed against a doorknob. I twisted it, pushing and pulling on the door. But it wouldn't move. I could hear the clown breathing behind me in the pitch dark.

I was trapped.

5

I gave the door another desperate shove, and it sprang open. Sunlight blinded me, but I didn't wait for my eyes to adjust. I sprinted down the stairs and kept running, as fast and as far as my legs would take me. I didn't stop to look where I was or who was around – but it seemed as though the fairground was empty. I kept pushing forward. My lungs felt ready to collapse. After I gained some distance, I paused to catch my breath. Sweat dripped down my neck.

Then I heard a sound that made the droplets of sweat on my back freeze into crystals of ice.

Someone was whistling behind me, a long, slow, creepy melody. I turned, and there he was. The clown, ambling towards me. He was dripping wet.

My mind spun. What if Trevor wasn't lying? What if the kidnapper really had escaped? What if this was him, coming for me? Mine could be the next face on a missing poster.

I wasn't going to wait to find out. I took off running again. I didn't even notice my surroundings. I just kept running. And running and running, until I could no longer hear the whistling.

Eventually I collapsed against the side of a building, my lungs on fire. With a deep breath, I peered around the side of the building. The clown wasn't in sight anymore. But neither was anyone else. I had no idea where I was. I couldn't hear any laughter or talking or joyous shouts. I couldn't see the Ferris wheel. I couldn't even smell any popcorn.

I pulled my phone from my pocket. "Great," I muttered, staring at the black screen. "It's dead."

I stood up and looked around. All that surrounded me were old, rusty tin buildings with no windows. They all looked the same, one after the other, surrounded by trees. It was like the buildings had been dumped down in the middle of a thick forest.

I knew I must still be in the fairground at least, because I hadn't passed any fences or gates. I turned back the way I came, keeping an eye out for any sign of the monstrous clown. But the path kept going in circles, weaving through the trees and leading me right back to where I'd started.

I decided to examine the buildings, hoping they could help me work out my location. *These must be storage sheds*, I thought as I inspected the garage doors. The thought gave me hope. If they were storage sheds, then eventually someone would come along to grab something or put something away. But, when I looked closer, I saw that most of them had thick, rusted padlocks on the doors. The locks looked like they hadn't been opened in a long time.

I flopped down against the wall of one building to organize my thoughts. Maybe I was just panicking. Maybe I'd missed another path leading back to the park.

I got to my feet and made my way along the wide gravel path, more slowly this time. The sunshine was gone. Clouds covered the sky, casting everything in a greyish-blue glow. I shivered. I knew I didn't have much time. The bus would be leaving soon. I didn't think Ms Bentley would leave me behind. But what if she did? I'd have to spend the night – or maybe the rest of my life – in this abandoned part of the amusement park. I would die here, and my bones would scorch under the sun.

Maybe they'll put my skeleton in the House of Horrors, I thought, laughing a little. But my laugh turned into a sob, which echoed back at me.

I wiped my eyes with my T-shirt and told myself to stop crying. I needed to come up with an action plan. But when I stopped crying, I could still hear my sobs ringing through the air.

But wait. That wasn't me crying. The cries sounded much higher-pitched and more sniffly than mine. They were coming from somewhere else.

I wasn't alone out here. Someone else was nearby. And someone else was crying.

"Hello?" I yelled. "Anyone there?"

The crying stopped for a moment. Then a voice called out, "Help! Help me!" The voice sounded like it belonged to a little girl.

What if it's a trick? I thought. But then I pushed the thought away and walked towards the sound.

"Help!" the voice called again, louder this time. I walked faster, making my way towards the voice. As I got close to the building that I thought the voice was coming from, I noticed there was no padlock on the door.

I pushed the door open and stuck my head inside. "Hello?" I said. "Are you in there?"

No answer.

I swung the door open wider and stepped inside.

Then I froze. The room was filled with hundreds of clowns. Hundreds! All staring at me with their painted smiles.

The door banged shut behind me. My legs gave out, and I crumpled to the ground.

A hand grasped my shoulder, and I knew this was the end. I was about to meet my biggest fear — *death by clown.*

6

"Help me." The voice seemed to come from someone right next to me.

I looked up and expected to see the clown, his face in my face, globules of spit glowing on his red smile. But when I turned around, I saw it was a little girl, eyes ringed in red, her nose dripping.

"Please," she sniffled.

I sat up and looked around. The room was filled with clowns, all right, but they weren't live clowns. Clown masks, clown heads, clown statues, clown signs, clown posters, everything and anything imaginable to do with clowns, lined the walls. I was in some nightmarish clown den. My heart started pounding.

"I'm lost," the little girl whispered. And then she scampered away into the shadows.

"Wait!" I cried, scrambling to my feet.

She ducked behind a clown statue and peered out at me. As I stepped towards her, she darted away again.

"I'll help you," I said. "But you have to come out!"

I wove my way between the clowns, looking for her. I heard a tiny giggle behind me. The little girl had her arms wrapped around a giant clown doll. She peeked around its head, giggled again and crawled under the row of shelves, dragging the doll behind her.

I was starting to feel frustrated, my nerves on edge. I decided to try something. I walked towards the door. "I'm leaving now!" I called.

"No! Stay!" she cried. She let go of the clown doll, ran towards me and clutched my leg.

I pried her fingers off my leg and grabbed her hand. "Let's go and find your parents," I suggested.

"OK," she whispered.

Then, from the corner of my eye, I saw something move. My stomach twisting, I scanned the rows of clown faces. All fake.

My gaze stopped on one mask. Its eyes glowed, looking eerily human. And then the eyes blinked.

"Who's there?" I shouted. I took a step closer to the mask. The eyes stared straight ahead, not blinking.

I must be seeing things, I told myself. *First a hundred live clowns. Now a mask with human eyes.* I scooted the little girl out of the door and slammed it shut behind us.

Outside, the sun was peeking through the clouds and casting a ray of light on the gravel path.

I was starting to feel a bit better. At least I wasn't out here alone.

"What's your name?" I asked the little girl.

"I'm Lucy, and I'm lost," she said.

"I'm Josh, and I'm lost too," I told her, smiling.

Lucy didn't smile. She just stared at me with her round, dark eyes. "I didn't want to leave him behind," she said.

"Who?"

"The clown."

I gulped. "The . . . doll?"

"He's not a doll. He's real."

Real? I looked back at the storage shed. Goosebumps ran up my arms. Was the kidnapper clown in there? Maybe he'd been about to kidnap Lucy when I turned up.

"Come on," I hissed, breaking into a jog. Lucy ran alongside me. Her legs pumped to keep up. Then she wrestled her hand from mine and came to a stop.

"I don't want to be lost!" she wailed.

"We can make this an adventure!" I panted. "And then we can tell our friends all about it."

"I want my mum!" Lucy screamed.

I patted her shoulder as she cried. "We won't find her unless you come with me," I told her. I pointed down the path that wound through the buildings, away from the clown shed. "Let's go this way."

I tried to sound confident, but I was suddenly even more afraid. Now I felt responsible for Lucy. I had another person depending on me. What if I couldn't get us out of here, and the kidnapper clown found us?

"So, how old are you, Lucy?" I asked as we walked, trying to sound cheerful.

"Five."

"And what do you like to do?"

"Nothing," she said. Then her lips started trembling. "I d-don't like being scared," she stuttered.

"I know," I said.

"You!" she said, suddenly sounding angry. "You're big! I bet you're not scared of anything!"

"I am," I admitted. "I'm scared of clo—" I started to say. Then I stopped. I didn't want to give her a clown phobia too. "Clams! I'm scared of clams."

Lucy giggled. "Clams?"

"Yes. They're just so . . . clammy!"

Pretty soon we were both laughing. Through our laughter, I thought I heard another deep laugh booming from the trees. But when I looked, no one was there.

7

Lucy chattered and even skipped a little as we continued on. I felt proud of myself for cheering her up. But we still had a problem. We had to get back to the park and get away from the clown, wherever he was. I didn't know if Trevor's story about the clown escaping prison was true, but I didn't want to find out.

"Balloon!" Lucy shrieked suddenly.

Before I had time to react, Lucy had wriggled her hand away from mine and was running towards the trees. "Stop!" I yelled, chasing after her.

In the wooded area behind one of the buildings, I saw a blue balloon rising out of the bushes. *How on earth could Lucy have seen a balloon from so far away?* I wondered as I clambered after her. Then I saw that the balloon was not stuck in the branches, as I'd thought. It was attached to someone – a clown.

He leaned down and held the balloon out to Lucy.

"Balloon!" she shrieked again, nearly tripping over her own two feet to get to the clown.

"No, Lucy, NO!" I roared. I was closing in on them now. But if I got close enough, the clown might grab me too. And then we'd both be doomed.

But I'd never forgive myself if I didn't save her.

I took a giant leap and grasped Lucy by the wrist, just as she touched the balloon string. I turned around and pushed my way through the trees, with Lucy close behind me. She was crying again, pointing to the sky. It was the balloon drifting above us. Lucy whimpered, "My balloon."

When we reached the gravel path, I looked back. The clown was still in the woods, watching. And now he had another balloon.

Lucy followed my gaze. "No!" I said, clapping my hands over her eyes. I couldn't take a chance that she'd run for a balloon again. "Let's go!" I pulled her along the gravel path, walking quickly in the direction I expected the park to be.

And then I heard it. *Crunch. Crunch.* The clown's footsteps on the gravel behind us. "Stop!" he boomed. And then the footsteps grew quicker. He was running now. Chasing us.

8

"Run!" I yelled to Lucy. "Run as fast as you can!"

She did, her little legs struggling to keep up with mine. I glanced back, and the clown was gaining on us. I knew Lucy couldn't outrun him. But I could.

I hardly knew Lucy, but I didn't want her to end up as clown food. "Faster, Lucy!" I begged.

"Why?" she gasped. "Why are we running?"

I didn't answer. I knew we were facing another problem. The path just led in circles. The clown could chase us around and around until we collapsed. I had to find another way. Maybe we could give him the

slip somehow. But we'd have to go off the path to lose him.

The path curved, and for a moment we were out of sight of the clown. "This way," I whispered, leading Lucy between two buildings towards a wooded area. A chain-link fence ran along the side of the woods. A hand-painted wooden sign read: *Danger! Keep Out.*

Danger? What could be more dangerous than the predator clown? With just a second's hesitation, I lifted Lucy over the fence, and she climbed down the other side. Then I climbed over. The fence rattled with my weight, and the sound was loud in the silent air. I hoped the clown didn't hear it.

"Let's tiptoe," I whispered. "We have to be very, very quiet."

"Why?" Lucy said in a whisper so loud it sounded like a shout.

I put my finger on my lips and stepped forward. Twigs splintered under my feet. We tiptoed along, Lucy's hand trembling in mine. She could sense my fear, and she was afraid too.

Up ahead, I saw something that gave me hope. A building loomed large and greyish through the trees. It looked like a house or an office building. But as we got closer, my hope plummeted. It wasn't a building. It was a huge concrete wall, too high to climb over. On the other side of the wall, I could hear traffic.

I couldn't believe it. We were so close to civilization. We were so close to someone who might save us. But we were separated by a thick wall.

I sank down against a tree, and Lucy flopped down beside me, frowning.

"Let's just wait here for a while," I said.

A tear rolled down her cheek. "This isn't a very fun adventure," she said.

Between the buzzing sounds of traffic, I could hear something else. *Crunch. Crunch. Crunch.*

The clown had followed us into the woods.

9

I looked up into the face of the clown, ready to meet my doom.

"Relax. It's not like I'm going to gobble you up or something," the clown said. I was shocked. From the clown's mouth came the voice of a girl. She sounded friendly.

The clown took off her wig and shook out long, blonde hair. Then she removed the clown mask and smiled down at us. Not a fake, painted smile, but a real one.

"I'm Maria," she said, holding out her hand for me to shake.

There was no way I was touching clown gloves, even if they were attached to a pretty girl. I got to my feet, still staring at the clown Maria. She was probably seventeen or eighteen years old. I couldn't believe that the clown of my nightmares was actually a teenage girl.

"I saw you wandering around by the storage sheds," Maria said. "I thought you must be lost. I wanted to help you, but you just kept running away!"

My racing heart finally slowed to a normal pace. Suddenly I felt foolish for being so scared. "I suppose I was just a little spooked," I told her. "Did you hear about the clown who kidnapped some kids?"

"I did!" she said. She lowered her voice. "And did you hear that he escaped this morning?"

I stiffened. So Trevor wasn't making it up.

The clown was out there, somewhere, waiting for his next victim.

"And he left behind a deflated balloon. Genius!" Maria let out a weird, deep laugh. I glanced at her. I didn't think it was very funny.

Lucy giggled and grabbed Maria's hand. "I love balloons," she said.

"I have lots back at the park," Maria said. "Let me show you the way."

"That would be great," I said. "My friends are probably looking for me."

Maria led the way through the woods and back to the gravel path that wound around the storage units. She pointed to another path leading away from the storage units. I couldn't believe I'd missed it in all of my wandering earlier. "This way," she said.

We made our way along the path. A gust of wind rattled the leaves on the trees around us.

I looked up. "Are you sure we're heading in the right direction?" I asked. The trees were getting more crowded, and it seemed to be getting darker.

"We're just taking a shortcut through the woods," Maria explained. "We'll be there in no time."

I nodded. Through the rattling leaves, I could hear faint shouts from the amusement park. I thought we must be getting closer.

As we walked, Maria told me about her job working as a clown. I noticed she kept pressing her cheeks with her fingers. *That's a strange nervous habit*, I thought.

"How long have you worked here?" I asked her.

"Oh, a couple of years," she said. "But it feels like forever."

"What made you want to become a—" I hesitated. The word still gave me the creeps.

Maria might've been a clown, but she was just a normal teenager.

"Why did I become a clown?" she said. "I needed a part-time job, and the amusement park was looking for people," she said. "I realized I love making kids laugh." She jiggled her hips and did a funny little clown dance. Lucy burst into giggles.

Maria stopped dancing and suddenly looked serious. "I don't make much money at the amusement park, though," she admitted. "I got another job this morning. . . ." She trailed off and looked at me, grinning.

"Oh?" I said. "What's your other job?"

Maria tugged on her cheeks again. Then she let out a long cackle. "At a pizza place!"

I stared in horror as she peeled off her skin and then her blonde wig. Underneath was her real face and her real orange hair.

The clown.

"Are you hungry? Hungry for pizza?" asked the clown, moving closer and flinging a deflated balloon on the ground. "I can always eat a slice!"

GLOSSARY

admission right or permission to enter

chatter talk about unimportant things

collapse fall down suddenly

eerily in a spooky or creepy manner

habitat natural place and conditions in which something lives

maniacally crazily

paved when a road or pavement is covered with a hard material such as concrete or asphalt

plummet drop sharply

slump sit down heavily and suddenly

turrets little towers, often at the corners of a building

FACE YOUR FEAR!

Now that you've read the story, it's no longer only inside this book. It's also in your brain. Can your brain help you answer the questions below?

1. Write a scene in the story from Sienna's point of view. What happens to her after she and Theo are separated from Josh?

2. Write a newspaper article about what happened in the amusement park during the story. How would you report on what happened to Josh and his friends?

3. Josh doesn't want his friends to know he is afraid of clowns. Have you ever hidden something about yourself from your friends? Why?

4. Did the ending of the book surprise you? Why or why not?

5. Write a story about what you think happens after the story ends. Do you think Josh and Lucy get away from the clown?

FEAR FACTORS

coulrophobia — the fear of clowns

No one could be afraid of clowns until there WERE clowns. The traditional clown with frizzy hair, white make-up and bright red nose started appearing at circuses in the 19th and 20th centuries. One reason clowns are disturbing is that their white faces remind us of ordinary human faces that have turned pale due to fear or surprise.

The Auguste Amusement Park in the story takes its name from a traditional type of clown: the auguste. The auguste, sometimes called a red clown because of its reddish make-up, was usually the butt of the jokes and pranks perpetrated by the clown with white make-up who was the star of the show. Someone has to take the pie in the face!

The Joker character from the Batman comics is one of the best-known clowns in popular culture. His white face, red lips and green hair were introduced to comic book readers in 1945, not long after April Fools' Day. The Joker is sometimes called "the Clown Prince of Crime".

Brain scientists believe that some people develop a phobia of clowns because of the so-called "uncanny effect". Uncanny means "beyond the ordinary" or "uncomfortably strange". Clowns are not quite human. Our brains know clowns are really people, but they don't look or behave like normal humans. So our brains get confused, and therefore frightened.

ABOUT THE AUTHOR

Jessica Gunderson grew up in a small town in North Dakota, USA. She has a bachelor's degree and an MFA in Creative Writing. She has written more than seventy-five books for young readers. Her book *Ropes of Revolution* won the 2008 Moonbeam Award for best graphic novel. She currently lives in Wisconsin, USA, with her husband and cats.

ABOUT THE ILLUSTRATOR

Mariano Epelbaum is a character designer, illustrator and traditional 2D animator. He has been working as a professional artist since 1996, and enjoys trying different art styles and techniques. Throughout his career Mariano has created characters and designs for a wide range of films, TV series, adverts and publications in his native country of Argentina. Mariano has also contributed to several children's books, including Fairy Tale Mix-ups, You Choose: Fractured Fairy Tales and Snoops, Inc.

It was very early. The house was quiet.
Fizzy Pop stretched and yawned.
Mum was still asleep and Fizzy knew
better than to wake her up too early
on a Saturday morning. Mum would
grumble and beg to be left alone. "I'm
exhausted, Fizzy," she'd say.

Fizzy reached into a drawer in her
bedside cabinet where she found a
slightly furry red jelly baby. "Yummy,"
she said, biting off the head and having
a good chew. Then she opened a book.
It was full of baby animals – kittens
and chicks and best of all, puppies.

"If I had a dog I wouldn't be so bored all the time," Fizzy thought to herself. But Mum had told her countless times that it was impossible. Who would feed it and walk it and clear up its stinky mess? They couldn't have one. No.

Still, it didn't stop Fizzy from hoping.
She grabbed some crayons and a
notebook and started to draw a picture
of her perfect pet. It was a golden dog
with a black nose and very curly hair.

Chapter Two

By the time Mum finally got out of bed, Fizzy was already dressed in a pirate costume and an orange tutu. While Mum made eggs and sausages, Fizzy's favourite Saturday morning breakfast, Fizzy skipped into the garden.

"Breakfast will be ready in ten minutes!" Mum called out.

"I won't be long!" Fizzy said. She had already eaten about fifty chewy sweets which she'd found hidden in various places around the house, so she wasn't hungry, but she didn't tell Mum that.

There was a hole in the garden fence which was big enough for Fizzy Pop to fit through if she crouched low. She crawled through into the next-door neighbour's garden.

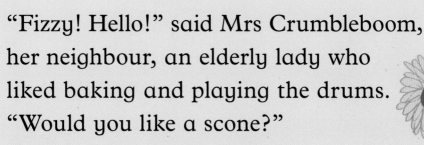

"Fizzy! Hello!" said Mrs Crumbleboom,
her neighbour, an elderly lady who
liked baking and playing the drums.
"Would you like a scone?"
"No thanks, Mrs Crumbleboom. Mum
is cooking."
"Ah. OK then,"
Mrs Crumbleboom
said, and suddenly,
she barked. Woof.
Just like that.

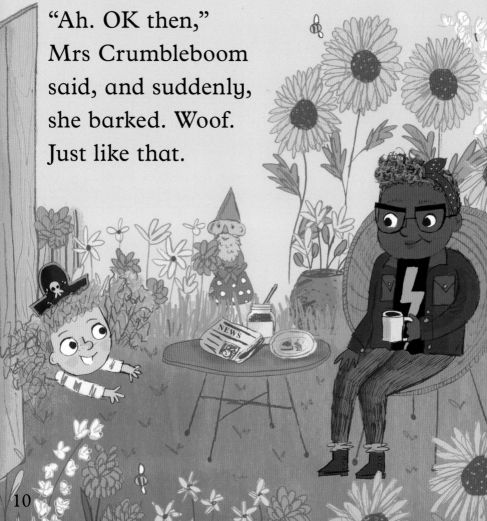

"Did you say something?" Fizzy said.
Mrs Crumbleboom barked again.

Fizzy wondered whether to get Mum.
Or maybe a doctor. Or a vet. But just
before she ran for help something
astonishing happened.

A golden dog with a black nose and
very curly hair came hurtling out of
Mrs Crumbleboom's kitchen, jumped up
on Fizzy, and began licking her face.

Chapter Three

"Get down, Bandit!" Mrs Crumbleboom shouted at the dog. She waved her hands but Bandit didn't seem to care and went on furiously licking Fizzy who had fallen to the ground in a fit of giggles.

"What a handful!" Mrs Crumbleboom
said. "He won't behave, you know."
"Where did he come from?" Fizzy
asked, sitting up and petting the dog.
She was sure she must have brought
him to life through her picture.

"My brother has gone to live in Spain and wasn't able to take poor Bandit, so I said I'd keep him." Mrs Crumbleboom shook her head. "He's lovely. It's just a lot of work."

CLICK!

Fizzy had an idea and smiled. "Yes,
I suppose it will be such hard work for
you caring for him all by yourself."
The dog had run up the garden now and
was peeing on Mrs Crumbleboom's herbs.
"Oh dear," Mrs Crumbleboom sighed.

Chapter Four

"And I suppose you'll have to stop baking," Fizzy said. The dog was now chewing Mrs Crumbleboom's gnome. "Yes," said Mrs Crumbleboom sadly. Fizzy Pop should have tried to comfort her neighbour, but instead she continued.

"And I suppose you'll have to give up drumming and devote yourself to picking up dog poo. A dog makes a lot of poo you know." As if he were listening, Bandit suddenly squatted and did what dogs do.

"My garden!" cried Mrs Crumbleboom, flopping into a garden chair and staring at Bandit with a worried expression. "What you need is someone to take that dog off your hands. And that person is me!" Fizzy pointed at herself, a pirate in an orange tutu.

"Oh, no," said Mrs Crumbleboom.
"Your mum would never allow it."
Fizzy got into trouble quite a lot, but
she was not usually a fibber. However,
she made an exception this once.

"Mum loves dogs," she said. "She told me this morning that we need a guard dog. You know, to growl at strangers."
"Really?" said Mrs Crumbleboom.
Fizzy stood up tall. "Come here, Bandit!" she called in a firm voice.

As soon as she'd said it, Bandit stopped snuffling in the bushes and came straight to Fizzy. He sat next to her and looked up admiringly. "Give me a paw," she said. And Bandit did.

"I'm excellent with animals," Fizzy
explained to Mrs Crumbleboom.
She was surprised herself at just how
excellent she seemed to be.
"You are," Mrs Crumbleboom said.
"So I can have him?" Fizzy asked.
"Yes please," said Mrs Crumbleboom.

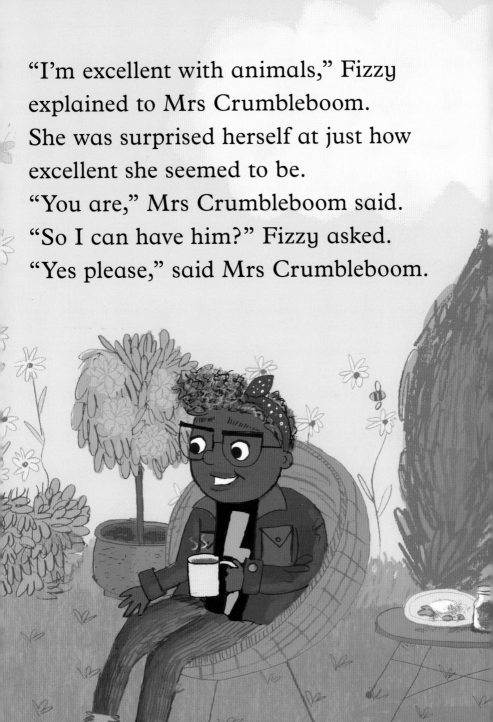

23

Chapter Five

The first problem was how Fizzy was going to get Bandit into the house without Mum noticing. Luckily, Bandit was a small dog. And even luckier, Mum had burned the sausages. The kitchen was filled with smoke, so she was busily waving a tea towel in the air.

Fizzy picked up Bandit, crept through the kitchen and dashed upstairs to her bedroom. Bandit barked but Fizzy Pop shook her head. "You must be quiet," she said. "If you're naughty, Mum will find you and send you away."

"Breakfast in five minutes!" Mum called up the stairs.

"Right, you hide under there," Fizzy said, pointing to her bed.

Bandit wagged his tail happily but didn't move so Fizzy had to push him. He peered out. He barked again. And out he came.

At that moment, Fizzy heard Mum's footsteps on the stairs.

"Oh no!" Fizzy said, and in one swift movement, she threw her duvet over Bandit and stood firmly between him and the doorway.

"Didn't you hear me calling?" Mum asked.

Fizzy stared at her. "Yes."
Mum sniffed the air and grimaced.
"What's that smell?"" she asked.
"Have you been eating cabbage?"
Fizzy wriggled from one foot to the
other, trying to make sure Bandit
was hidden behind her. "No,"
she said.

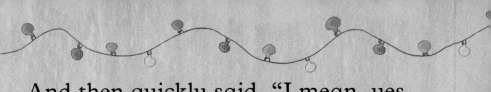

And then quickly said, "I mean, yes.
That's what the smell is. Sorry." She
tried to look embarrassed.

"Why are you squirming like that?"
Mum continued. "Do you need the loo?"

"No," Fizzy said. "I mean, yes!" She
really wasn't very good at lying.

"Well go to the loo, then straight down to breakfast. And afterwards let's air this room and tidy up a bit."
With that, Mum turned around and clomped downstairs.
Fizzy pulled off the duvet. Bandit grinned. "I'll have to find a better hiding place," Fizzy said.

Chapter Six

Fizzy Pop opened her school bag and put Bandit into it next to her pencil case. She zipped it up, leaving a gap for his head, and put him carefully into her wardrobe feeling pleased with herself. "Mum won't look in there," she said.

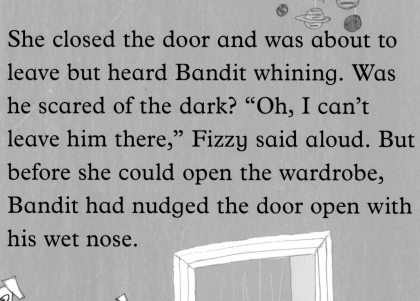

She closed the door and was about to leave but heard Bandit whining. Was he scared of the dark? "Oh, I can't leave him there," Fizzy said aloud. But before she could open the wardrobe, Bandit had nudged the door open with his wet nose.

He tumbled out into the room, and lay on the carpet panting. Then he barked loudly. He seemed to really like barking. But at least he didn't look too upset with her.

Fizzy needed a better idea.

Even if she could persuade Bandit to stay in the wardrobe, how would she stop him from making a noise? She couldn't exactly drag the television upstairs and turn it on to muffle the sound. Mum would definitely notice.

So Fizzy went into the bathroom and looked around. Finally she put Bandit into the laundry basket and covered him with dirty tights and t-shirts.

"Stay," she whispered, but he obviously wasn't fond of smelly clothes and jiggled himself free.

Fizzy huffed. "Bandit," she pleaded, picking him up and popping him into the bath. She covered him in a towel. But he shook it off. And then he did the same thing with a bath mat and a blanket from her bedroom and a coat and a whole toilet roll.

"OK, OK," Fizzy said. "But where can I hide you?" She looked at the toilet. "Should I?" she asked herself. She looked at Bandit. He was very small. He probably couldn't swim. And if he somehow got flushed into the sewers by mistake, that would be awful.

"Better not," she said. She picked up
Bandit and carried him into Mum's
bedroom.

"There," she said, sitting Bandit on the
bed with an old slipper to chew. "Try
to sleep. I'll be back in five minutes.
Don't pee on anything."

"Fizzy Pop, if you aren't down these stairs in three seconds…" Mum hollered.

"Coming!" Fizzy shouted and she tiptoed out of Mum's bedroom.

Chapter Seven

Breakfast went on forever. Mum kept piling Fizzy's plate with overcooked eggs and charred sausages and then started nagging her about her spellings for Monday. Fizzy heard a bang from upstairs and began to swing her legs nervously.

"Can I leave the table?" she asked politely. Just then she heard a whine. Next it would be a howl. And a bark. "Please, Mum."

"I was thinking," Mum said, ignoring her question, "should we get a pet? With the summer coming it might be nice."

"What?" asked Fizzy, completely confused. Her mother hated animals. She liked things tidy. She didn't like poo.

"A pet," Mum repeated. "You know. An animal you keep at home. Might be good company. And I know you've been wanting one for ages."

"I know what a pet is, Mum," Fizzy said, and grinned. "Thing is," she began, ready to tell Mum all about Mrs Crumbleboom and Bandit. Suddenly, from upstairs, she heard the unmistakeable sound of a toilet flushing.

"Argh!" Fizzy Pop screamed. It was so loud, Mum almost toppled off her chair. "What is it?" Mum screamed back. Fizzy jumped up and ran. "It's Bandit. I think he's flushed himself down the toilet."

She took the stairs two at a time.
She hurtled into the bathroom, and
there, by the toilet bowl, was Bandit,
completely soaked but totally alive, his
long tongue licking the toilet seat.

Fizzy ran to him and hugged him tightly. "Thank goodness you're alright," she said. "I'm so sorry I tried to hide you."

Mum was behind her. "Fizzy," she said, "I'm guessing you have something to tell me."

Fizzy looked up at Mum, a cheeky smile on her face. "Look how quickly I found us a pet," she said. "His name is Bandit. And it's OK, you don't have to thank me. You're very, very welcome."